MYSTERIOUS UNIVERSE

SUNDARAM DUBEY

Contents

Foreword   *v*

1. Vision Of - James Hopwood Jeans   1

2. Was There Life On Mars??   14

3. Black Holes   19

4. Time Travel   23

Foreword

An eminent mathematician and astrophysicist Sir James Jeans in his book – The Mysterious Universe – gives us a glimpse of the littleness of the Earth, our home in space, a microscopic fragment of a grain of sand when measured up against the total substance of the universe.
A few stars are known which are hardly bigger than the Earth, but the majority are so large that hundreds of thousands of earths could be packed inside each and leave room to spare; here and there we come upon a giant star large enough to contain millions of millions of earths. And the total number of stars in the universe is probably something like the total number of grains of sand on all the seashores of the world.

The vast multitude of stars is wandering about in space. A few form groups which journey in company, but the majority are solitary travellers. And they travel through a universe so spacious that it is an event of an almost unimaginable rarity for a star to come anywhere near to another star. For the most part, each voyage is in splendid isolation, like a ship on an empty ocean. In a scale model in which the stars are ships, the average ship will be well over a million miles from its nearest neighbour, whence it is easy to understand why a ship seldom finds another within hailing distance.

It is believed, nevertheless, that some two thousand million years ago this rare event took place, and that a second star, wandering blindly through space, happened to come within hailing distance of the sun. Just as the moon raises tides on the earth, so this second star must have raised tides on the surface of the sun. But they would be very different from the puny tides which the small mass of the moon raises on our oceans; a huge tidal wave must have travelled over the surface of the sun, ultimately forming a mountain of prodigious height, which would rise ever higher and higher as the cause of disturbance came nearer and nearer. And, before the second star began to recede, its tidal pull would become so powerful that this mountain was torn to pieces and threw off small fragments of itself, much as the crest of a wave throws off spray. These small fragments have been circulating around their parent sun ever since. They are the planets, great and small, of which our earth is one.

This is his vision refered from him into this book.

1

VISION OF - James Hopwood Jeans

Born into a family of journalists in 1877, James Hopwood Jeans was a precocious child who learned how to read and count at an early age. In 1896 he left his childhood home in London for Trinity College at the University of Cambridge. After completing his studies in mathematics and physics in 1903 and briefly working as a lecturer in mathematics, he accepted a position as a professor of applied mathematics at Princeton University in 1905. He stayed there for four years before returning to Cambridge to become the Stokes Lecturer in applied mathematics.

James Hopwood Jeans (1877–1946) was a prolific physicist and science popularizer. (Courtesy of the AIP Emilio Segrè Visual Archives.)

During the first half of his scientific career, Jeans did research in statistical mechanics and blackbody radiation. He is perhaps best known today for the Rayleigh–Jeans law—originally derived by Lord Rayleigh in 1900 and amended by Jeans in 1905—which describes the radiation intensity of a blackbody at a given temperature as a function of wavelength. The law was derived in a classical framework and is valid only for long wavelengths. For shorter wavelengths, the function goes to infinity; that problem became known as the ultraviolet catastrophe.

Jeans tried to avoid the ultraviolet catastrophe within a classical framework by introducing additional hypotheses, but he eventually concluded that the attempted solution was a dead end. In his Report on Radiation and the Quantum-Theory, written for the Physical Society of London in 1914, Jeans argued that quantized energy, as suggested by Max Planck in 1900, was necessary. The report aided in the development and acceptance of quantum physics in the UK.

From 1914 on Jeans shifted his research from the very small to the very large—from atoms and molecules to stars and the universe. He received the University of Cambridge's Adams Prize for his essay "Problems of cosmogony and stellar dynamics," which was published as a book in 1919. Jeans went on to serve as the honorary secretary of the Royal Society of London for a decade, all while keeping up his prolific research on stellar dynamics. He published more than 35 astronomical papers between 1913 and 1928. One of his last technical publications was the book Astronomy and Cosmogony, in which he summarized his astrophysical research and attempted to survey the field generally. After 1929 Jeans diverted his energy to science popularization.2

The Einstein boom

Physics came to the forefront of the British public imagination during the final decade of Jeans's career as a researcher. Astronomers Arthur Eddington and Frank Dyson organized expeditions to test Albert Einstein's general theory of relativity during the solar eclipse of May

1919 (see the article by Daniel Kennefick, Physics Today, March 2009, page 37). After the results were made public in November 1919, the world experienced what has been described as a "relativity circus."3 Almost overnight Einstein became a global superstar and an icon of genius, international science, and the modern world (see the article by Paul Halpern, Physics Today, April 2019, page 38).

Demand was growing for texts explaining the new, revolutionary picture of the universe. Eddington wrote one of the earliest book-length popularizations, Space, Time and Gravitation: An Outline of the General Relativity Theory, published by Cambridge University Press in 1920. It was favorably but not widely reviewed. The book sold well and was reprinted several times during the 1920s.

Einstein, too, wrote a popularization of relativity, Über die spezielle und die allgemeine Relativitätstheorie (Relativity: The Special and General Theory), published in German in 1916 and translated to English in 1920. But he lacked Eddington's gift for marketing physics to laypeople; his book was dry and did not sell as well. The slew of books on relativity that followed initiated what literary scholar Elizabeth Leane calls the "Einstein boom" in popular physics publishing4 in the 1920s and 1930s.

As early as 1922, interest in relativity seemed to be waning. Magazines and journals claimed that Einstein was "last season" (Nouvelle Revue Française, January 1922) and that "even philosophers have had enough of relativity" (Mind, October 1922; both quotes are from reference 5, page 56). But two developments saved the genre. First, most popularizers widened their scope to include the other modern-physics revolution, quantum mechanics. Second, they discussed the new physics' significance and implications for philosophy and spirituality.

Although popularizations of relativity continued to appear—some of them written by famous writers such as Bertrand Russell and John W. N. Sullivan—the books that dominated the market took the broader view. Literary scholar Michael Whitworth singles out three books, all published by Cambridge University Press, as particularly influential: Alfred North Whitehead's Science and the Modern World (1925), Eddington's The Nature of the Physical World (1928), and Jeans's The Mysterious Universe (reference 5, page 62). Of those, The Mysterious Universe was by far the most successful.

The making of a popularization

The Mysterious Universe was not Jeans's first popular science book. Sydney C. Roberts, the secretary at Cambridge University Press, persuaded Jeans to write one in 1929. The result, The Universe Around Us, became an immediate best seller and sold more than 11 000 copies in the first few months alone (reference 6, page x). In comparison, Eddington's The Nature of the Physical World sold only around 10 000 copies in the UK in over a year.7 But both those figures pale in comparison with those of The Mysterious Universe.

In 1930 Allen Ramsay, vice chancellor of the University of Cambridge, invited Jeans to deliver the Rede Lecture, the university's prestigious annual public address whose roots go back to the 16th century. Encouraged by the success of The Universe Around Us, Jeans agreed to publish an expanded version of the lecture as a book, The Mysterious Universe. It was published on 5 November, the day after Jeans gave his highly anticipated talk. An editor at the Times, Harold Child, reported that "the whole office is buzzing about Jeans." In anticipation of its popularity, Cambridge University Press printed 10 000 copies for the initial release. But those were not enough. "For the next few weeks," Roberts says, "our chief concern was to keep The Mysterious Universe in stock" (reference 6, page xi).

Shortly after the Rede Lecture, the BBC aired six weekly lectures, "The Stars in Their Courses," by Jeans. The first one was promoted on the 14 November cover of the BBC's weekly magazine The Radio Times. The following week's issue featured an article by Richard Church—with the eye-catching title "Einstein: Why don't we boil him in oil?"—about Jeans and the changing attitudes toward scientists.8 That media attention boosted the sales of The Mysterious Universe, and by the end of 1930, the book had sold 70 000 copies in the UK. The sales remained high into 1931, and by the end of that year, The Mysterious Universe had been reprinted eight times along with a second, revised edition (reference 5, page 71).

Before settling on the title, Jeans considered two alternatives: "The Wasting Universe" and "The Shadowland of Modern Physics" (reference 7, page 52). Those titles hint at different aspects of Jeans's vision of the universe and at his intentions beyond explaining science for laypeople. The philosophical ambitions of The Mysterious Universe are apparent already in the first few pages of the first chapter, ominously named "The Dying Sun."

After emphasizing "the littleness of our home in space" and the isolation of most stars as they wander "blindly through space," Jeans reveals that the universe provokes "something akin to terror" in him: "We find the universe terrifying because of its vast meaningless distances, terrifying because of its inconceivably long vistas of time which dwarf human history to the twinkling of an eye, terrifying because of our extreme loneliness, and because of the material insignificance of our home in space—a millionth part of a grain of sand out of all the sea-sand in the world" (reference 1, pages 1 and 3).

Questions about the meaning of life amid that abundant meaninglessness preoccupy Jeans and inspire him to use poetic language. "Is this, then, all that life amounts to," he asks, "to stumble, almost by mistake, into a universe which was clearly not designed for life, and which, to all appearances, is either totally indifferent or definitely hostile to it, to stay clinging on to a fragment of a grain of sand until we are frozen off, to strut our tiny hour on our tiny stage with the knowledge that our aspirations are all doomed to final frustration, and that our achievements must perish with our race, leaving the universe as though we had never been?" But rather than turning to religion for an answer, Jeans turns to science: "Astronomy suggests the question, but it is, I think, mainly to physics that we must turn for an answer" (pages 11–12).

The answer, however, is not straightforward

On the one hand, thermodynamics suggests that the universe is heading inexorably toward dissolution. The eventual heat death of the universe—a uniform, homogeneous state in which life is impossible—was a popular idea in the Victorian era.9 For Jeans, that fate was as certain as anything in science, although in the last chapter, he does allow for the possibility that the idea may prove to be mistaken. The approaching heat death inspired Jeans's sense of life's meaninglessness. In a universe bound for destruction, we live on "a fragment of a grain of sand" (page 11) next to that dying Sun.

The 1919 solar eclipse provided the first experimental evidence of the theory of general relativity. Using glass photographic plates, Arthur Eddington and Andrew Crommelin imaged the eclipse, as shown here after restoration and modern processing. When stars were close to the Sun—and visible during the eclipse—they appeared displaced due to the bending of light by the Sun's gravity, as predicted in general relativity. The observation created demand for popular science books explaining the topic. (Courtesy of ESO/ Landessternwarte Heidelberg-Königstuhl/F. W. Dyson, A. S. Eddington, and C. Davidson.)

To Jeans, physics suggests that planets and life are exceedingly rare. The mechanisms of planetary formation were unknown at the time, and Jeans used his platform to promote his own theory, the tidal theory originally formulated in 1917. In it, a star happened to pass by the Sun some 2 billion years ago, and that near collision created huge stellar tidal waves, which ejected fragments of solar matter into space—and thus the planets were formed. Jeans estimated that near collisions between stars are extremely rare, and as a result, so are planets and life. That rarity adds to his sense of "our extreme loneliness."

On the other hand, according to Jeans, physics also holds the key to understanding the universe and ourselves. In the last chapter, "Into the Deep Waters," Jeans develops his vision of the philosophical implications of emerging physics. He suggests that we are similar to the cave dwellers in Plato's allegory of the cave: We see and study the shadows of reality, not reality itself. But through physics and mathematics, we are beginning to glimpse reality.

Jeans emphasizes that science is incomplete and that we may yet see "the river of knowledge" turn in unexpected ways. But he contends that physics has shown that some ideas we took for granted are almost certainly wrong. In particular, Jeans argues that we must give up science's long-cherished materialistic and mechanical worldview, which posits that nature operates like a machine and consists solely of material particles interacting with each other. The "age of mechanical science had passed," Jeans says, but we still have "a bias towards mechanical interpretations" (pages 98 and 135). The new physics is counterintuitive and reveals a universe more mysterious than expected.

What, then, does science say about the nature of the universe? Jeans uses modern science in his speculations, but he cautions that he is "a stranger in the realms of philosophical thought" (page viii). And those speculations are what many critics interpreted as Jeans going off the deep end.

Jeans embraces a variant of metaphysical idealism. Not only does the universe begin "to look more like a great thought than like a great machine" (page 137), but some kind of active agent seems to be involved: "If the universe is a universe of thought, then its creation must have been an act of thought" (pages 133–134). Although Jeans does not think that such a creative act of thought necessarily had humans or human emotions in mind, he does posit the existence of some kind of creator—a "Great Architect" who appears to be a "pure mathematician" (page 122). And if true, then the mind "no longer appears as an accidental intruder into the realm of matter; we are beginning to suspect that we ought rather to hail it as the creator and governor of the realm of matter" (page 137).

The upshot of Jeans's philosophy is that the sensations of terror and alienation described in the first chapter may be unwarranted. As it evolves, life approaches ultimate reality: "Those inert atoms in the primaeval slime which first began to foreshadow the attributes of life were putting themselves more, and not less, in accord with the fundamental nature of the universe" (page 138). And we humans, with our capacity for mathematical thought, are more in accord with the fundamental nature of the universe than any other life-form on planet Earth. In other words, physics leads us toward, not away from, a deity. In the end, physics provides our souls with a home in the cosmos in the form of metaphysical intimacy with the Creator.

The descent of Jeans

As sales of The Mysterious Universe skyrocketed, critics started opining on Jeans's vision of the universe. The press homed in on the speculative qualities of the last chapter and tended toward sensationalist interpretations. The Daily Herald, for example, framed Jeans's conclusions as science versus religion, as evidenced in the title "Scientist challenges the churches: Mankind just an accident" (reference 5, page 70).

The first edition of The Mysterious Universe came out in 1930 and sold 70 000 copies in the UK by the end of that year. In the book, Jeans explains to a lay audience the latest research on quantum mechanics and general relativity with a philosophical bent. (Courtesy of Laura Massey/ Alembic Rare Books.)

Scientists and highbrow critics started to distance themselves from The Mysterious Universe, in large part because the book's success provoked them to air their concerns publicly. Physicist Herbert Dingle, writing in Nature, expressed admiration for Jeans's ability to explain physics in lay terms but criticized his philosophical speculations. Dingle argued that since Jeans had the means to reach large numbers of laypeople "who seek guidance in matters of philosophy and religion," Jeans had a responsibility not to overstep the boundaries of science. Dingle did acknowledge the importance of putting forth hypotheses in science, but not hypotheses that "pose as the sole prophets of God." And in that regard, Jeans failed.

Dingle wrote, "we feel strongly that he is darkening counsel, not by words without knowledge, but, much more dangerously, by knowledge without equivalent balance of judgement."10 Many scientists agreed with Dingle's assessment.

Philosophers also criticized Jeans. Ludwig Wittgenstein told his students that he loathed The Mysterious Universe and charged it with "a kind of idol worship, the idol being Science and the Scientist."11 In her 1937 book Philosophy and the Physicists, L. Susan Stebbing criticized Jeans and Eddington for invoking emotions when explaining science. She also argued that Jeans's understanding of idealism and materialism were outdated and thus his attempt to explore the "'philosophical implications' of the new physics" resulted in "cloudy speculations" rather than substantial insights.12

The broader philosophical landscape in the UK was changing at the time. Idealism had dominated academic philosophy starting in the 1860s. But shortly after the turn of the 20th century, philosophers G. E. Moore and Bertrand Russell started to attack idealism, and by 1930 it was rare in the British philosophical world. Most philosophers eschewed the idealists' emphasis on metaphysics and questions about the nature of being and turned instead to logic, positivism, and linguistic analysis. While idealism was common among physicists in their popularizations in the 1920s—Eddington and Whitehead, the other best-selling authors at the time, also had idealist views—the general trend among philosophers was to turn away from it.13

The scientific and philosophical critiques of Jeans and idealism affected the entire genre of popular physics books. Although many popularizers kept publishing, the hype and the excitement surrounding the genre had waned. Eddington's and Whitehead's idealist views had not met with as much resistance in the 1920s; it was Jeans's book that brought the criticism to the fore and spelled the end of idealism in popular science. Whitworth comments that the "very blurring of science, philosophy and art, which had stimulated the science books of the mid-1920s, was now seen by philosophers and scientists alike as an unwelcome breaching of disciplinary boundaries" (reference 5, page 72).

Popular science did not disappear. But following World War II and the creation of the nuclear bomb, it transformed as scientific institutions and journalists sought to restore public faith in science. As a result, much popularization focused on the social implications and practical applications of science. Space exploration and astronomy remained popular—for example, the works of Fred Hoyle and Arthur C. Clarke14—but grand philosophical and poetic narratives didn't attract similar levels of public attention as The Mysterious Universe did for a few decades.

Finally at home in the cosmos?

This year marks not only the 90th anniversary of The Mysterious Universe but also the 40th anniversary of Carl Sagan's Cosmos, the best-selling popular science book and television series, which helped create the modern celebrity scientist.15 Sagan guided readers and viewers through the world of modern science and created a grand narrative in which humanity is the product of natural processes reaching all the way back to the Big Bang. Similar to Jeans, Sagan not only explained science, he also used it to address existential questions. Also like Jeans, Sagan posited a connection between human beings and the universe. In the opening sequence of the first episode, standing on a cliff by the sea, he says, "The cosmos is also within us. We're made of star stuff. We are a way for the cosmos to know itself."

Carl Sagan (1934–96), the prominent science popularizer, on the set of his 1980 TV show Cosmos. In his show and book of the same name, Sagan injects existential questions into his scientific discussion, similar to James Jeans. (Courtesy of Science History Images/Alamy Stock Photo.)

After the enormous success of Sagan and Cosmos, popular science books that present grand narratives and address existential questions have had a sustained market. But popularizers rarely express philosophical views of Jeans's flavor; idealism has broadly remained out of favor since the 1930s. Instead, contemporary popularizers typically promote some version of naturalism, which philosopher David Papineau defines as the view that "reality is exhausted by nature, containing nothing 'supernatural', and that the scientific method should be used to investigate all areas of reality, including the 'human spirit.'"16 That view often has the implication that meaning and purpose are human inventions with no objective existence.

In his 2016 best-selling book The Big Picture, cosmologist Sean Carroll develops and supports that aspect of naturalism: "Purpose and meaning in life arise through fundamentally human acts of creation, rather than being derived from anything outside ourselves. Naturalism is a philosophy of unity and patterns, describing all of reality as a seamless web."17 In other words, people construct meaning in an inherently meaningless universe. And engaging in science is one of the primary ways of making life meaningful.

Contemporary readers of popular science may find naturalism almost self-evidently true—of course we create meaning and project it onto the universe; of course meaning and purpose do not exist objectively. But Jeans's extension of idealism to physics was similar. He developed his views when idealism was prevalent among his fellow popularizers and had been commonplace in academic philosophy for decades, just as naturalism is today. Could the feeling of naturalism's self-evidence say more about our moment in time than the universe itself? Our scientific models and explanations may be naturalistic, but does that mean that ultimate reality is too?

2

Was there life on mars??

As of this writing, there is no proof of life on Mars now or at any time in the planet's history. No Martians, no spiders or girls with mousy hair (sorry David Bowie), no microbes, no tardigrades ... no life on Mars. Despite that, there is plenty of hope within the science community that there could have been life on the Red Planet at one time. One potential sign that Mars could have supported some microbes is that models of its ancient atmosphere show evidence that microbes could have lived there about 3.7 billion years ago – coincidentally, when microbes were beginning to come alive in Earth's oceans. However, while our microbes were learning how to survive and spread, these new models show that these simulated Martian creatures did something that resulted in their planet-wide extinction ... and it was due to the same deadly condition we're now encountering today on Earth – climate change. Did Martian microbes really terminate their own existence? Could the same thing happen on Earth?

Could this be what life on Mars looked like?

"We think Mars may have been a little cooler than Earth at the time, but not nearly as cold as it is now, with average temperatures hovering most likely above the freezing point of water. While current Mars has been described as an ice cube covered in dust, we imagine early Mars as a rocky planet with a porous crust, soaked in liquid water that likely formed lakes and rivers, perhaps even seas or oceans."

In a press release from the University of Arizona, Regis Ferrière, a professor in the university's Department of Ecology and Evolutionary Biology and a senior author of a paper on the research published in Nature Astronomy, sets the stage for building a model for what life on Mars might have looked like in the Noachian period 3.7 billion years ago when Mars was being bombarded by meteorites and asteroids on both land and in what could have been a large amount of surface water. The planet would also have had temperate climate and a thin but viable atmosphere made of carbon dioxide and hydrogen. That would be a hostile environment for Earth microbes accustomed to oxygen in the atmosphere and hydrogen in the water. However, there is one Earth microbe that lives in such a hostile place – the methanogenic microbes found around the deep submarine hydrothermal vents at the bottom of the oceans. Could early Mars have been inhabited by similar methanogenic microbes? The model says yes ... but.

"Our goal was to make a model of the Martian crust with its mix of rock and salty water, let gases from the atmosphere diffuse into the ground, and see whether methanogens could live with that. And the answer is, generally speaking, yes, these microbes could have made a living in the planet's crust."

The model used spectroscopic measurements of rocks exposed on the Martian surface to predict that the water on the planet was extremely salty. The computer software then added various atmospheric compositions to predict temperatures at the surface and in the crust for each possibility. Each iteration created an ecosystem which the model would then evaluate to determine whether the methanogenic microbes would have been able to survive and, more importantly, how the microbes would have affected the environment over time. The good news is ... this methanogenic life thrived at a level just a few inches below the Martian surface at the beginning. The bad news is ...

"The problem is that even on early Mars, it was still very cold on the surface, so microbes would have had to go deeper into the crust to find habitable temperatures. The question is how deep does the biology need to go to find the right compromise between temperature and availability of molecules from the atmosphere they needed to grow?"

According to Boris Sauterey, a former postdoctoral fellow and study co-author, the model revealed what was causing the temperature change on the Martina surface ... unfortunately and quite surprisingly, it was the methanogenic microbes themselves! The simulation shows the microbes removing hydrogen from the thin atmosphere at a very fast rate – so fast that some models showed the atmosphere being completely changed in just 10,000 years, with others stretching it to hundreds of thousands of years. By "changed," the researchers mean cooled down ... down to the point of being covered with ice – a situation that was unsuitable for microbes used to a warm hydrogen-filled atmosphere. What would you do if you were one of these gasping, shivering Martian microbes?

"The problem these microbes would have then faced is that Mars' atmosphere basically disappeared, completely thinned, so their energy source would have vanished and they would have had to find an alternate source of energy. In addition to that, the temperature would have dropped significantly, and they would have had to go much deeper into the crust."

With no warmth and no energy source, the ancient methanogenic microbes dug themselves deeper and deeper into the surface of Mars, proving that tiny microbial brains in desperate situations will – at least in computer models – make very bad decisions. While they may have been a bit warmer as they moved away from the frozen surface, they were also moving away from their only source of hydrogen energy. As these microbes dug deeper and deeper, they may have come to a grim realization – they were digging their own graves. Too late to change their tiny minds and unable to change their physiology to utilize another energy source – if there even was one – the methanogenic microbes finally succumbed to a self-inflicted extinction.

Was Mars once thriving with microbes?

Or did they? Remember, this was only a model. The real proof will be to find fossilized microbes – but that will require drilling far deeper below the Martian surface than any Mars probes have dug so far. There is also a very remote possibility that some of these ancient methanogenic microbes survived – they could be the source of traces of methane detected in today's Martian atmosphere by satellites or the cause of the strange 'alien burps' of methane detected by NASA's Curiosity rover. The day humans set foot on the Red Planet can't come soon enough.

One more thing ... the model shows the extinction of these Martian life forms was self-inflictied by overusing the atmosphere and creating climate change. Sound familiar? It does to Boris Sauterey, who says this may be why we haven't found any other life in the universe yet.

"So it's possible that life appears regularly in the Universe. But the inability of life to maintain habitable conditions on the surface of the planet makes it go extinct very fast. Our experiment takes it even a step farther as it shows that even a very primitive biosphere can have a completely self-destructive effect."

Is Earth the only place in the universe where life hasn't self-destructed? Is this a good reason to make sure we're not on the same path as the Martian methanogenic microbes? Perhaps David Bowie was musing not about life on Mars but about life across the universe when he sang"

3
Black holes

Don't let the name fool you: a black hole is anything but empty space. Rather, it is a great amount of matter packed into a very small area - think of a star ten times more massive than the Sun squeezed into a sphere approximately the diameter of New York City. The result is a gravitational field so strong that nothing, not even light, can escape. In recent years, NASA instruments have painted a new picture of these strange objects that are, to many, the most fascinating objects in space.

Intense X-ray flares thought to be caused by a black hole devouring a star. (Video)

Watch the Video

The idea of an object in space so massive and dense that light could not escape it has been around for centuries. Most famously, black holes were predicted by Einstein's theory of general relativity, which showed that when a massive star dies, it leaves behind a small, dense remnant core. If the core's mass is more than about three times the mass of the Sun, the equations showed, the force of gravity overwhelms all other forces and produces a black hole.

A video about black holes.
Watch the video

Scientists can't directly observe black holes with telescopes that detect x-rays, light, or other forms of electromagnetic radiation. We can, however, infer the presence of black holes and study them by detecting their effect on other matter nearby. If a black hole passes through a cloud of interstellar matter, for example, it will draw matter inward in a process known as accretion. A similar process can occur if a normal star passes close to a black hole. In this case, the black hole can tear the star apart as it pulls it toward itself. As the attracted matter accelerates and heats up, it emits x-rays that radiate into space. Recent discoveries offer some tantalizing evidence that black holes have a dramatic influence on the neighborhoods around them - emitting powerful gamma ray bursts, devouring nearby stars, and spurring the growth of new stars in some areas while stalling it in others.

One Star's End is a Black Hole's Beginning

Most black holes form from the remnants of a large star that dies in a supernova explosion. (Smaller stars become dense neutron stars, which are not massive enough to trap light.) If the total mass of the star is large enough (about three times the mass of the Sun), it can be proven theoretically that no force can keep the star from collapsing under the influence of gravity. However, as the star collapses, a strange thing occurs. As the surface of the star nears an imaginary surface called the "event horizon," time on the star slows relative to the time kept by observers far away. When the surface reaches the event horizon, time stands still, and the star can collapse no more - it is a frozen collapsing object.

Astronomers have identified a candidate for the smallest-known black hole. (Video)

Watch the Video

Even bigger black holes can result from stellar collisions. Soon after its launch in December 2004, NASA's Swift telescope observed the powerful, fleeting flashes of light known as gamma ray bursts. Chandra and NASA's Hubble Space Telescope later collected data from the event's "afterglow," and together the observations led astronomers to conclude that the powerful explosions can result when a black hole and a neutron star collide, producing another black hole.

Babies and Giants

Although the basic formation process is understood, one perennial mystery in the science of black holes is that they appear to exist on two radically different size scales. On the one end, there are the countless black holes that are the remnants of massive stars. Peppered throughout the Universe, these "stellar mass" black holes are generally 10 to 24 times as massive as the Sun. Astronomers spot them when another star draws near enough for some of the matter surrounding it to be snared by the black hole's gravity, churning out x-rays in the process. Most stellar black holes, however, are very difficult to detect. Judging from the number of stars large enough to produce such black holes, however, scientists estimate that there are as many as ten million to a billion such black holes in the Milky Way alone.

On the other end of the size spectrum are the giants known as "supermassive" black holes, which are millions, if not billions, of times as massive as the Sun. Astronomers believe that supermassive black holes lie at the center of virtually all large galaxies, even our own Milky Way. Astronomers can detect them by watching for their effects on nearby stars and gas.

This chart shows the relative masses of super-dense cosmic objects.

Read the full article

Historically, astronomers have long believed that no mid-sized black holes exist. However, recent evidence from Chandra, XMM-Newton and Hubble strengthens the case that mid-size black holes do exist. One possible mechanism for the formation of supermassive black holes involves a chain reaction of collisions of stars in compact star clusters that results in the buildup of extremely massive stars, which then collapse to form intermediate-mass black holes. The star clusters then sink to the center of the galaxy, where the intermediate-mass black holes merge to form a supermassive black hole.

4

Timetravel

Everyone can travel in time(opens in new tab). You do it whether you want to or not, at a steady rate of one second per second. You may think there's no similarity to traveling in one of the three spatial dimensions at, say, one foot per second. But according to Einstein(opens in new tab)'s theory of relativity(opens in new tab), we live in a four-dimensional continuum — space-time — in which space and time are interchangeable.

Einstein found that the faster you move through space, the slower you move through time — you age more slowly, in other words. One of the key ideas in relativity is that nothing can travel faster than the speed of light(opens in new tab) — about 186,000 miles per second (300,000 kilometers per second), or one light-year per year). But you can get very close to it. If a spaceship were to fly at 99% of the speed of light, you'd see it travel a light-year of distance in just over a year of time.

That's obvious enough, but now comes the weird part. For astronauts onboard that spaceship, the journey would take a mere seven weeks. It's a consequence of relativity called time dilation, and in effect, it means the astronauts have jumped about 10 months into the future.

Traveling at high speed isn't the only way to produce time dilation. Einstein showed that gravitational fields produce a similar effect — even the relatively weak field here on the surface of Earth(opens in new tab). We don't notice it, because we spend all our lives here, but more than 12,400 miles (20,000 kilometers) higher up gravity is measurably weaker— and time passes more quickly, by about 45 microseconds per day. That's more significant than you might think, because it's the altitude at which GPS satellites(opens in new tab) orbit Earth, and their clocks need to be precisely synchronized with ground-based ones for the system to work properly.

The satellites have to compensate for time dilation effects due both to their higher altitude and their faster speed. So whenever you use the GPS feature on your smartphone or your car's satnav, there's a tiny element of time travel involved. You and the satellites are traveling into the future at very slightly different rates.

Navstar-2F GPS satellite. (Image credit: USAF)

But for more dramatic effects, we need to look at much stronger gravitational fields, such as those around black holes(opens in new tab), which can distort space-time(opens in new tab) so much that it folds back on itself. The result is a so-called wormhole, a concept that's familiar from sci-fi movies, but actually originates in Einstein's theory of relativity. In effect, a wormhole(opens in new tab) is a shortcut from one point in space-time to another. You enter one black hole, and emerge from another one somewhere else. Unfortunately, it's not as practical a means of transport as Hollywood makes it look. That's because the black hole's gravity would tear you to pieces as you approached it, but it really is possible in theory. And because we're talking about space-time, not just space, the wormhole's exit could be at an earlier time than its entrance; that means you would end up in the past rather than the future.

Trajectories in space-time that loop back into the past are given the technical name "closed timelike curves." If you search through serious academic journals, you'll find plenty of references to them — far more than you'll find to "time travel." But in effect, that's exactly what closed timelike curves are all about — time travel

HOW IT WORKS

How It Works is the action-packed magazine that's bursting with exciting information about the latest advances in science and technology, featuring everything you need to know about how the world around you — and the universe — works.

There's another way to produce a closed timelike curve that doesn't involve anything quite so exotic as a black hole or wormhole: You just need a simple rotating cylinder made of super-dense material. This so-called Tipler cylinder is the closest that real-world physics can get to an actual, genuine time machine. But it will likely never be built in the real world, so like a wormhole, it's more of an academic curiosity than a viable engineering design.

Yet as far-fetched as these things are in practical terms, there's no fundamental scientific reason — that we currently know of — that says they are impossible. That's a thought-provoking situation, because as the physicist Michio Kaku is fond of saying, "Everything not forbidden is compulsory" (borrowed from T.H. White's novel, "The Once And Future King"). He doesn't mean time travel has to happen everywhere all the time, but Kaku is suggesting that the universe is so vast it ought to happen somewhere at least occasionally. Maybe some super-advanced civilization in another galaxy knows how to build a working time machine, or perhaps closed timelike curves can even occur naturally under certain rare conditions.

An artist's impression of a pair of neutron stars - a Tipler cylinder requires at least ten. (Image credit: NASA)

This raises problems of a different kind — not in science or engineering, but in basic logic. If time travel is allowed by the laws of physics, then it's possible to envision a whole range of paradoxical scenarios(opens in new tab). Some of these appear so illogical that it's difficult to imagine that they could ever occur. But if they can't, what's stopping them?

Thoughts like these prompted Stephen Hawking(opens in new tab), who was always skeptical about the idea of time travel into the past, to come up with his "chronology protection conjecture" — the notion that some as-yet-unknown law of physics prevents closed timelike curves from happening. But that conjecture is only an educated guess, and until it is supported by hard evidence, we can come to only one conclusion: Time travel is possible.

A party for time travelers

Hawking was skeptical about the feasibility of time travel into the past, not because he had disproved it, but because he was bothered by the logical paradoxes it created. In his chronology protection conjecture, he surmised that physicists would eventually discover a flaw in the theory of closed timelike curves that made them impossible.

In 2009, he came up with an amusing way to test this conjecture. Hawking held a champagne party (shown in his Discovery Channel program), but he only advertised it after it had happened. His reasoning was that, if time machines eventually become practical, someone in the future might read about the party and travel back to attend it. But no one did — Hawking sat through the whole evening on his own. This doesn't prove time travel is impossible, but it does suggest that it never becomes a commonplace occurrence here on Earth.

The arrow of time

One of the distinctive things about time is that it has a direction — from past to future. A cup of hot coffee left at room temperature always cools down; it never heats up. Your cellphone loses battery charge when you use it; it never gains charge. These are examples of entropy(opens in new tab), essentially a measure of the amount of "useless" as opposed to "useful" energy. The entropy of a closed system always increases, and it's the key factor determining the arrow of time.

It turns out that entropy is the only thing that makes a distinction between past and future. In other branches of physics, like relativity or quantum theory, time doesn't have a preferred direction. No one knows where time's arrow comes from. It may be that it only applies to large, complex systems, in which case subatomic particles may not experience the arrow of time.

Time travel paradox

If it's possible to travel back into the past — even theoretically — it raises a number of brain-twisting paradoxes — such as the grandfather paradox — that even scientists and philosophers find extremely perplexing.

Killing Hitler

A time traveler might decide to go back and kill him in his infancy. If they succeeded, future history books wouldn't even mention Hitler — so what motivation would the time traveler have for going back in time and killing him?

Killing your grandfather

Instead of killing a young Hitler, you might, by accident, kill one of your own ancestors when they were very young. But then you would never be born, so you couldn't travel back in time to kill them, so you would be born after all, and so on ...

A closed loop

Suppose the plans for a time machine suddenly appear from thin air on your desk. You spend a few days building it, then use it to send the plans back to your earlier self. But where did those plans originate? Nowhere — they are just looping round and round in time.

Looper' Clocks Evils Of Time Travel

Time travel capabilities fall into the Mob's hands in the upcoming thriller. Includes MIT professor Max Tegmark and senior SETI astronomer Seth Shostak talking about the feasibility of time travel.